In Cahoots With My Boots

Sanya Whittaker Gragg

Illustrated by Stephanie Hider

Paperback ISBN: 978-1-7365353-3-2
Hardcover ISBN: 978-0-578-84360-5

Illustrations by Stephanie Hider (www.stephisdoodling.com)
Book design by Sarah E. Holroyd (https://sleepingcatbooks.com)

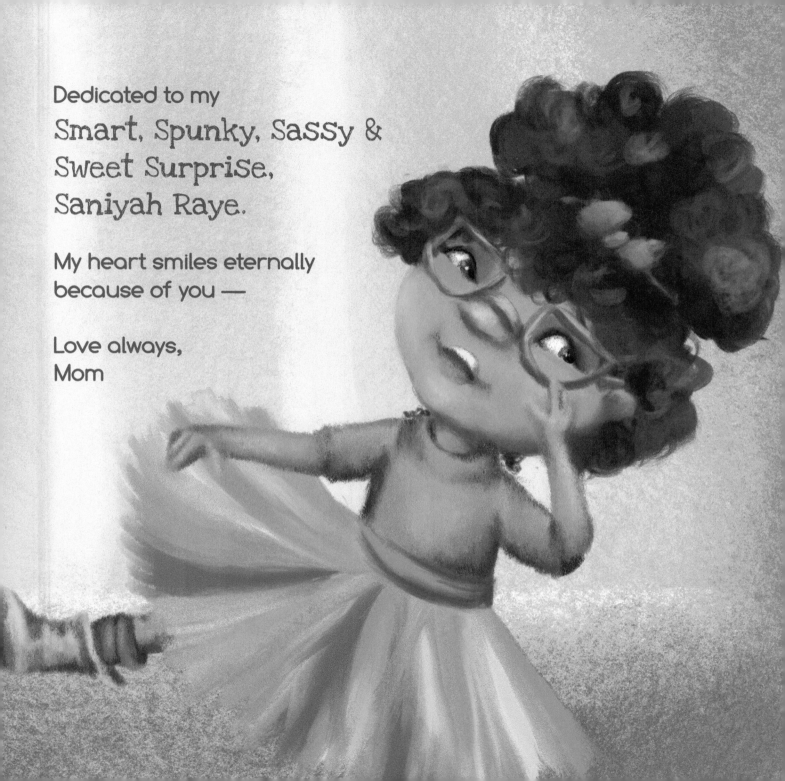

Dedicated to my
Smart, Spunky, Sassy &
Sweet Surprise,
Saniyah Raye.

My heart smiles eternally
because of you —

Love always,
Mom

I LOOOOOOVE

to wear my boots!

EVERY.
SINGLE.
DAY.

My boots are like my best friends.

And because of them, I never feel scared or alone.

Come a little closer and let me explain.

Ya see...some kids have stinky binkies.

Some have fluffy blankets.

Some have snuggly teddy bears.

But me...

Oh yeah! Oh yeah!

Oh yeah yeah yeah!

It's just

ME and

MY boots!

Mommy says that it's too hot to wear them in the summer-time.

But I still wear them with my shorts because...

WELL...

WHY NOT?

There's just something about the way I feel when I slide them onto my feet.

It's like a big warm hug from Mommy and I never want it to end.

When I wear my boots I feel...

Hmmm...what's that word when you really believe in yourself?

CONNNNNN-FI-DENT?

YES! That's it!

My boots make me feel super duper CON-FI-DENT!

Like I can do ANYTHING I put my mind to!

I don't even have to raise up on my tippy toes to feel tall

and proud
and strong
and smart
and amazing!

Because whenever I wear my boots,

I am ALL THAT and more!

My boots make me feel like I'm on top of the world!

No...no...I'm Princess of the Universe!

No...I'm Queen of the Galaxy!

YES! THAT'S IT!

I am Queen of the Galaxy...
to Infinity and Beyonnnnd!

Today I start big kids' school

But guess what the rule book said?!

NO BOOTS ALLOWED!
(GASP)

But I'm not worried because I remember what my Granny once said.

"Cupcake,"...(She calls me that because we always make the strawberry kind when she visits.)

Anyway...she said,

"Cupcake, some rules are just meant to be broken!"

So, on this first day of school I want to make her proud!

With my head held high, I strut down the sidewalk like a **proud peacock** with big beautiful feathers.

Oh YEAH! I'M STYLIN!!

And I'M CON-FI-DENT!

Even Annie, the coolest girl in kindergarten, gave me a wink and a high five!

And a fist bump from red-haired Flint when he saw my puddle splash.

I love the **Squish Squash** sound with every single step.

SQUISH SQUASH SQUISH SQUASH

I enter the school and proudly stomp down the hallway.

I turn the corner and see my new teacher staring from a distance.

Her laser focused eyes are looking right down at my feet.

And boy, I can tell she does NOT share my **good fashion sense!**

I can't really remember exactly what happened next.

All I know is some way, somehow,

I am now sitting on my mat with these ridiculous looking, pink velcro thingamajigs on my feet.

ARRRRRGGGGHHHH!

I'm pretty mad now!

But I also feel scared.

And alone.

How can I finish the day without my boots?

They always make me feel tall,

and proud

and strong

and smart

and amazing.

Now ALL those feelings are GONE!

My tummy feels all in knots and my hands are sweaty.

My legs feel like jello.

The teacher asks me to stand and say my name.

My mind is blank.

OH NO! What IS my name?

I NEED my boots, LADY!

They make me feel

CON-FI-DENT!

I take a deep breath.

Everyone is waiting.

I close my eyes.

I hear snickering.

And then, I imagine my beautiful, sparkly, snuggly boots back on my feet where they belong.

I exhale.

I feel calm.

I feel happy.

And yes, CON-FI-DENT.

Slowly, my eyes open.

"My name is SA-NI-YAH!" I exclaim.

Yes! That's it!

HOOORAHH!

My friends cheer me on!

I DID IT! I really did it!

And I feel tall,

and proud

and strong

and smart

and amazing!

Today I learned that no matter what
I'm wearing,

When I dig deep inside, I can still feel

CON-FI-DENT!

As soon as I got in mom's car in the pick-up line, guess what was waiting for me in the backseat?

YESSSSSSSS!

Oh yeah! Oh yeah!

Oh yeah yeah yeah!

It's just ME and MY boots!

Together. Forever.

Lightning Source UK Ltd.
Milton Keynes UK
UKHW052240310521
384683UK00002B/34

9 780578 843605